Dedicated:

To my Dad and
all the kids who do not have a dad.

When my daddy died, I cried. And then I prayed to God to help me with the hard times I have.

When my daddy died, I thought of all the fun times we had together. We played basketball with each other in the basement and outside.

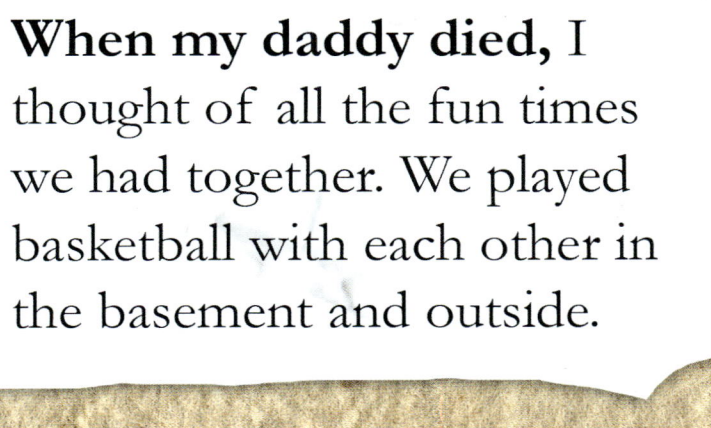

When my daddy died, I missed watching baseball, basketball and football games with him. He took us to the Green Bay Packers Family Night Game every year.

When my daddy died, I missed him taking me and my brother Jordan to school every day and stopping to get Pop Tarts on Fridays from the gas station.

When my daddy died, I thought of him always coming to my activities for school. He was congratulating me on a job well done for my Christmas concert!

When my daddy died, I thought about him reading Bible stories to all of us every night. I liked how Daddy told the stories in a silly voice! He was trying to sound like the people in the stories!

When my daddy died, I wanted him to take me to church and get donuts. Church is very important to my family.

When my daddy died, I thought that other kids should be grateful for their dads because life is short. Even if you are one hundred years old.

When my daddy died, I felt sad for my mom. She is very lonely and sad without my dad.

When my daddy died, I felt sad that I did not have him anymore. My mom thought it was a good idea to talk to a counselor.

When my daddy died, I wanted him to come down from Heaven and say goodbye.

When my daddy died, I thought about my last day with him. We drove to Minnesota for 10 hours with my mom. We ate pizza, salad and breadsticks. That's my dad's favorite!

When my daddy died, I remembered Daddy taking a picture of our feet because he thought we had long, funny toes like him!

When my daddy died, I missed him taking all of us on a walk, almost every day.

When my daddy died, I wanted everyone to go to Heaven and have faith in Jesus. I hope you will believe in Jesus too. If you would like to invite Jesus to be your Savior, please say this prayer.

Jesus, come into my heart and forgive me of all my sins. I believe that Jesus is real because he was born of the virgin Mary and He died on the cross for our sins. Jesus rose from the dead and now sits at the right hand of God. I believe in the Father God, Jesus and the Holy Ghost. Some people say the Holy Spirit. In Jesus name I pray. Amen!

                                              I'm going to Heaven!